Published by Gmür Verlag
Zachary and the Great Potato Catastrophe copyright © Gmür Verlag 2018
Text copyright © Junia Wonders 2018
Illustrations copyright © Gmür Verlag 2018
All rights reserved.

The moral right of the author and illustrator has been asserted.

ISBN 978-3-907130-00-1

www.juniawonders.com

For my playful boys
Junia Wonders

For my human and my furry family
Giulia Lombardo

This is based on an *almost* true story.
The name of the main character
has been changed to protect his identity.
The events mentioned in this book
have been told *almost exactly* as they occurred.

Under the floorboards
of a small bakery
lived a clever little rat
by the name of *Zachary*.

All day long he slept
with the smell of pastry:
pastries of all kinds
that smelled oh, so **tasty!**

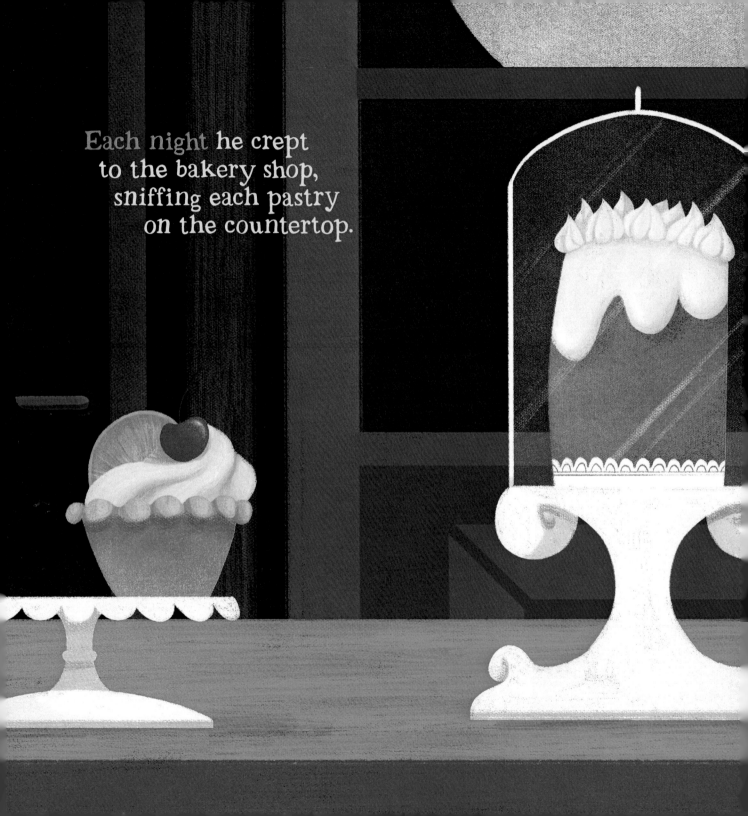

Each night he crept
to the bakery shop,
sniffing each pastry
on the countertop.

He ate one pastry;
that was his rule.
He **never** took seconds;
he wasn't a *fool*.

One pastry was enough,
and he didn't leave crumbs.
He didn't share, either,
with any of his chums.

His chums would beg
for a nibble or a taste.

But he'd say, "Go away!"
And they'd leave in haste.

You see, Zachary knew
if he ate more than one,
the baker would notice
and he'd come undone.

So he stuck to his rule
and lived *all alone*,
happy and content
in his own little zone.

strawberry jam

One night he saw a sack
that made his eyes pop.
Inside were potatoes
from bottom to top.

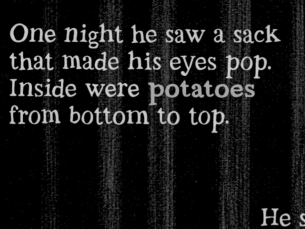

He sniffed and nibbled one
and thought it was tasty.
It tasted quite *different*
from his everyday pastry.

"The baker won't **know** if I take one of these," he said as he rolled a **potato** with ease.

The following night
he crept up once more
to grab two potatoes
to add to his store.

His stash kept growing,
but he didn't stop there.
When his chums came to visit,
he **still** refused to share.

What his chums said fell on deaf ears.
He thought potatoes lasted for years.

He kept on hoarding
till there were none.
Then he said to himself,

"My work here is done!"

Zachary admired his potatoes with pride!

potatoes all around,

potatoes by his side.

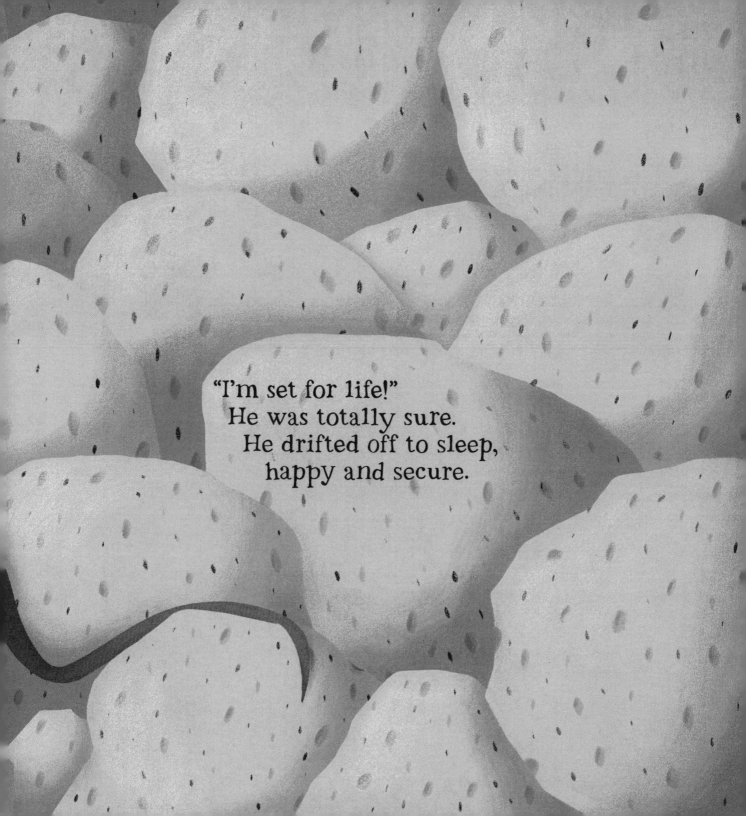

"I'm set for life!"
He was totally sure.
He drifted off to sleep,
happy and secure.

The days turned to weeks
as Zachary slept.
Waking only to eat
the **potatoes** he kept.

One not-so-fine day,
one he'd never forget,
Zachary woke
to **sudden regret**.

On the floor above him
was a commotion so loud.
"Where are my POTATOES?"
cried the baker to his crowd.

LOUR

Nobody knew,
so the baker had to look.
Guess what he found?
The hole to **Zachary's nook!**

Are there **rats** in my bakery?
the baker wondered.
How did this happen?
the baker pondered.

Crrrrrrrk!

Crrrrrk!

CRRRRRRRK!

The floors were ripped out.
Underneath were potatoes
that were starting to sprout.

The baker was surprised
when he saw the lone rat.
He tried to **squash** Zachary
with a very big vat.

Zachary panicked,
didn't know what to do.
He tried to run away,
but his feet felt like **glue**.

In the nick of time,
he managed to **escape**.
The baker was shocked;
his mouth hung agape.

Zachary ran as fast as he could.
He didn't dare stop and left for good.

Now Zachary was *clever*,
so he found a new nook
down in the sewers,
where **no one** would look.

It was under a **brewery**
filled with used-up grain.
He **welcomed** his chums;
it became their domain.

Zachary learned
that life could be **sweet**.
Sharing with chums
made life a treat.

The clever little rat
by the name of *Zachary*
lived a long, happy life
under the brewery.

Books by Junia Wonders

A sweet tale about **unconditional love!**

A wonderful & whimsical autumn tale!

An adorable rhyming tale of **bravery** and **hygiene**—with a little sprinkle of **magic!**

The **paperback** and **hardcov**
editions are available
Amazon and Barnes&Nob

Join *Junia's* VIP list at **www.juniawonders.co**

Made in United States
North Haven, CT
08 September 2022

23874900R00022